THE PRECIOUS GIFT

A NAVAHO CREATION MYTH

by Ellen Jackson   illustrated by Woodleigh Marx Hubbard

Simon & Schuster Books for Young Readers

Acknowledgments:
Lucille, Michele, David, Emily, and Ellen:
It has been a pleasure working with you,
and I would like to thank you for all the
fine work you have put into creating this
book with me. — W. M. H.

SIMON & SCHUSTER BOOKS FOR YOUNG READERS
An imprint of Simon & Schuster Children's Publishing Division
1230 Avenue of the Americas, New York, New York 10020
Text copyright © 1996 by Ellen Jackson
Illustrations copyright © 1996 by Woodleigh Marx Hubbard
SIMON & SCHUSTER BOOKS FOR YOUNG READERS is a trademark
of Simon & Schuster.
Designed by Lucille Chomowicz
The text of this book is set in Gill sans bold
The illustrations are rendered in gouache
Manufactured in the United States of America
First Edition
10 9 8 7 6 5 4 3 2 1
Library of Congress Cataloging-in-Publication Data
Jackson, Ellen B., 1943–
The precious gift: a Navaho creation myth by Ellen Jackson;
illustrated by Woodleigh Hubbard
p.   cm.
Summary: A retelling of part of a Navaho creation and evolution
myth in which of all the animals the lowly snail alone is responsible
for bringing pure water to the new land.
1. Navaho Indians—Folklore   2. Tales—Southwest, New.   3. Snails—
Folklore. [1. Snails—Folklore.   2. Navaho Indians—Folklore.
3. Indians of North America—Folklore.   4. Folklore—
Southwest, New.] I. Hubbard, Woodleigh, ill.   II. Title.
E99.N3J27   1996   398.2'0979045243089972—dc20
[E]   94-16709 CIP   AC
ISBN 0-689-80480-6

To my wonderful writing group:

Francess Lantz

Lou Lynda Richards — E. J.

To my mother and my nephew Jarret,

two wondrous gifts in my life. — W. M. H.

When the first people came from the underworld, it is said they came up through a reed in the ocean. Then they swam to land. Tired and thirsty, they looked around for something to drink.

But the new land was dry and parched. The sun shone fiercely, and the wind blew hard, swirling dust and grit over the mesas. First Man asked everyone, but no one had thought to bring any water.

"If I had only one drop of water," said First Man, "I could make a stream, a river, even a lake. Someone must go back and bring us fresh water."

"We will go," said Beaver and Otter.
So First Man gathered some shells and fashioned a
flask. Then he took a piece of coral and made a stopper.
Finally, he hung the flask around Otter's neck with a
cord of rainbow.

Otter and Beaver dove into the ocean. They swam to the bottom and walked on the ocean floor until they came to a beautiful valley. Everywhere sea lilies swayed gracefully, and scarlet starfish glittered in the sand.

It was so lovely that Otter and Beaver forgot their task. They began to gather flowers, roots, and vines. Soon they were covered from head to tail with growing things.

First Man was waiting on the beach when Otter and
Beaver came out of the water. They could hardly
waddle to shore with all their ocean treasures.

"Look, First Man!" they chattered. "Aren't these
beautiful? We found them in a valley and—"

"But where's the water flask?" asked First Man.

Otter and Beaver hung their heads.

"We must have left it behind," they said.

First Man sighed.

"You can keep your vines and lilies," he said.
"But you have chosen your future. From now on,
you will live in the swampy areas of lakes and
never know the pleasure of clear, fresh water."

"Who will go now?"
asked First Woman.
"We'll go find the flask and
bring back some water,"
said Frog and Turtle.

So Frog and Turtle dove into the ocean. They walked along the bottom until they came to the beautiful valley. There they found the water flask with a hermit crab perched on top.

Frog tied the flask on Turtle's back and they trudged on for a long time.

"Oh, my poor back is aching," said Turtle. "I can't take another step with this heavy thing on top of me. You go on without me, Frog. I'll wait here."

So Frog took the flask and walked on. He walked and walked and walked.

Turtle stayed behind and rested. Beside him grew a sticky plant. Turtle broke off a piece of the sticky plant and chewed it until he had made a kind of glue. Then he glued some shells together and put them on his back.

"Ah, that's better," he said. "With this suit I'll be able to carry the water flask."

Meanwhile, Frog was still walking. He had walked so far that his shoulders had sunk below his knees, and his eyes were starting to bulge. At last he found a gurgling spring of water.

"This is as far as I can go," he said. "It will have to do."

He filled the flask and started back.

By the time Frog returned, Turtle had glued together a shellplate for his front side to match the one on his back. Frog and Turtle then began the long journey home.

First Woman was on the beach waiting for Frog and
Turtle. When they came out of the water, she almost
didn't recognize them. Frog was all hunched over, and
Turtle was wearing a suit of shells.

"Where is the water?" asked First Woman.

"Oh, yes. I have it right here," said Turtle, handing
the flask to First Woman.

First Woman uncorked the flask and poured a little of the water into her hand. It was muddy and full of bugs. Frog and Turtle hung their heads.

First Woman sighed.

"You can keep your suit of shells," she said to Turtle. "But you and Frog have chosen your future. Because you put dirty water in the flask, you will both dine on bugs and live where the water is muddy and unclear."

And with that she turned away.

"Is there no one who will bring us back some water?" cried First Man and First Woman. None of the animals spoke up. They were all afraid to go.

"Let me try," said a quiet voice.

"You?" cried all the animals, for it was Snail who had spoken.

"Yes. I'll go back to our old home and bring us clear, fresh water," said Little Snail with determination.

Snail tied the water flask on her back. She dove into
the ocean. Then she crawled and crawled until she
found the reed that led back to the underworld. Down,
down she went, back to the world the people had left
behind.

At last Snail found a bubbling brook where the water
looked sweet and fresh. She tasted it to be certain.
Then she filled the water flask and rose to the top of
the ocean.

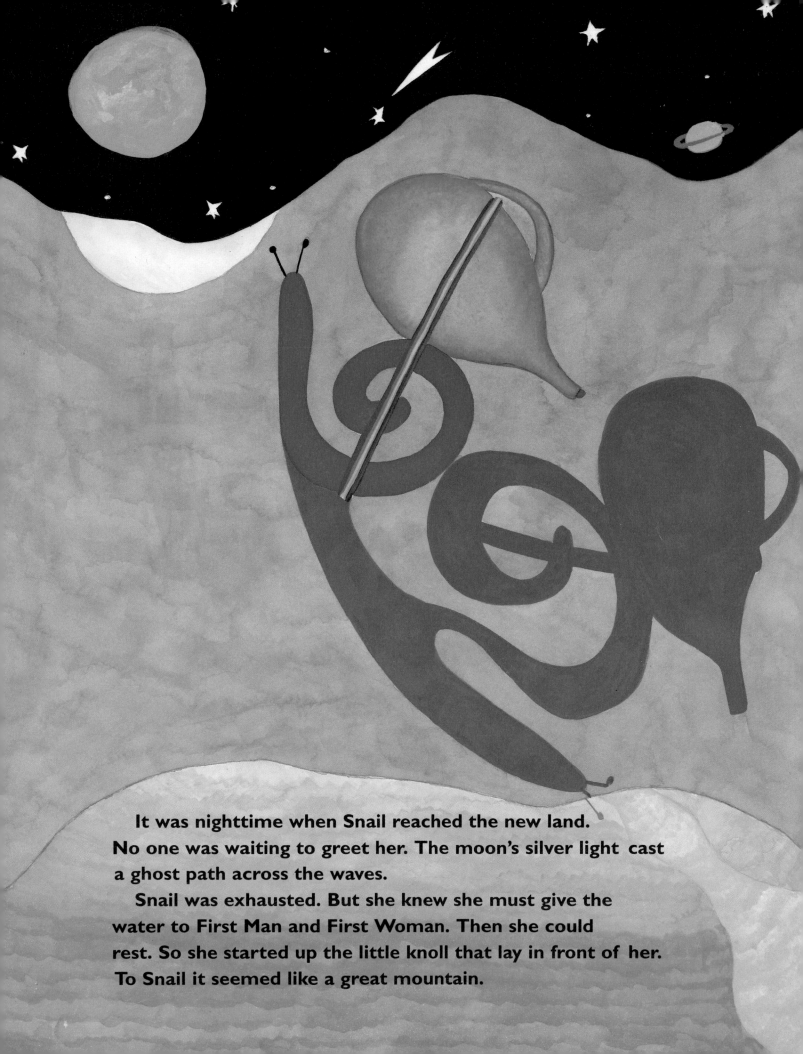

It was nighttime when Snail reached the new land.
No one was waiting to greet her. The moon's silver light cast
a ghost path across the waves.

Snail was exhausted. But she knew she must give the
water to First Man and First Woman. Then she could
rest. So she started up the little knoll that lay in front of her.
To Snail it seemed like a great mountain.

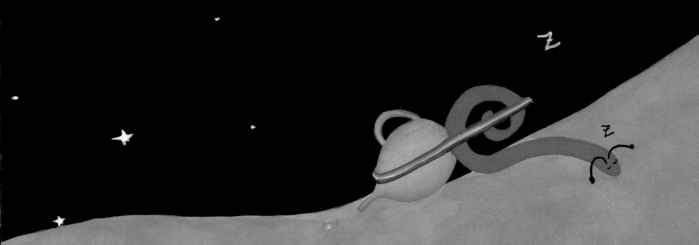

Slowly, slowly she crawled. The water flask dragged
on the ground behind her. A hole began to wear
through the bottom. Snail didn't hear the gurgle, gurgle
of the water leaking out onto the ground.

At the top of the hill, Snail stopped to rest. Soon she
was fast asleep.

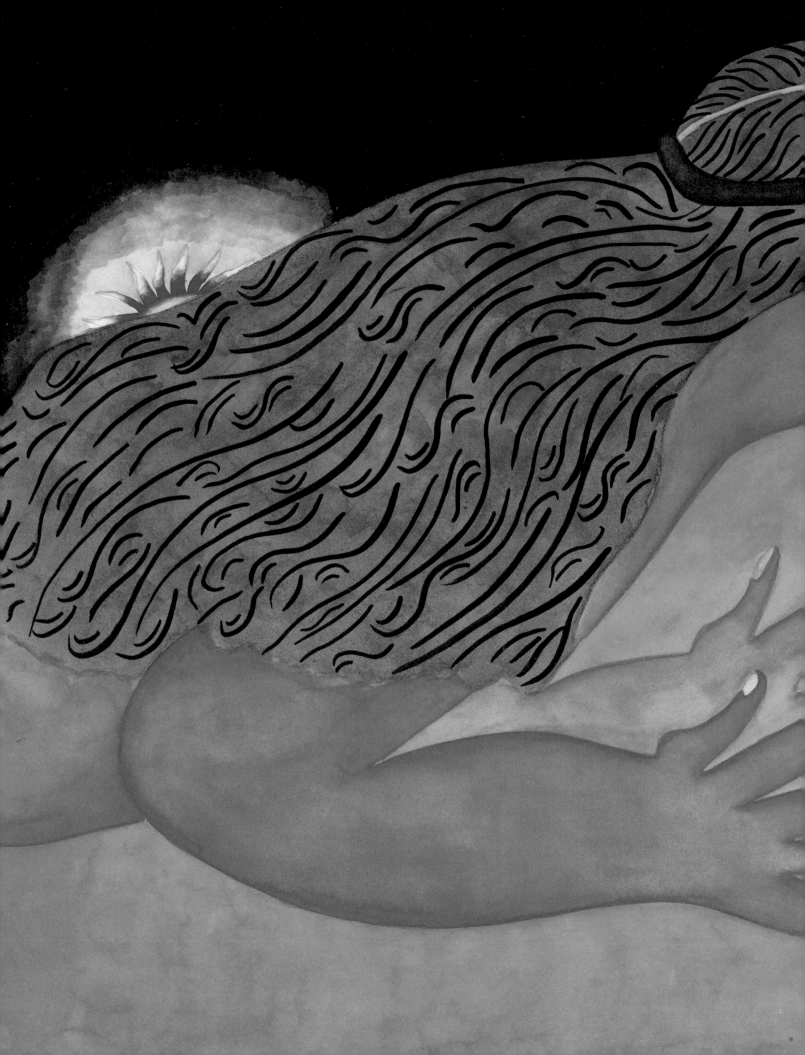

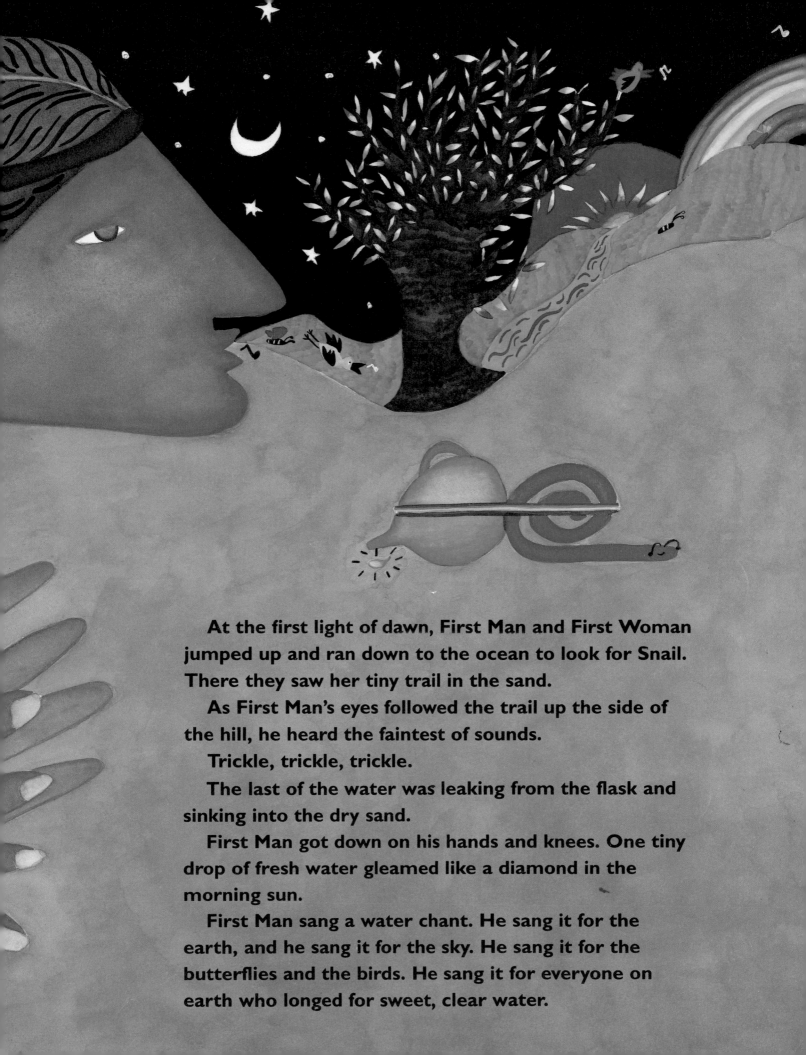

At the first light of dawn, First Man and First Woman jumped up and ran down to the ocean to look for Snail. There they saw her tiny trail in the sand.

As First Man's eyes followed the trail up the side of the hill, he heard the faintest of sounds.

Trickle, trickle, trickle.

The last of the water was leaking from the flask and sinking into the dry sand.

First Man got down on his hands and knees. One tiny drop of fresh water gleamed like a diamond in the morning sun.

First Man sang a water chant. He sang it for the earth, and he sang it for the sky. He sang it for the butterflies and the birds. He sang it for everyone on earth who longed for sweet, clear water.

The drop of water began to grow. First it became a stream, and then a raging river.

When Snail heard the sound of the river, she woke up and crawled down the hill.

"Snail," said First Man, "here is my gift for your good work. You may keep the water flask, and in the future you will carry it on your back and it will be a home for you."

"And here is my gift," said First Woman. "Whenever you crawl about, you'll leave a silvery, moist trail. And everywhere, when people see your trail, Little Snail, they will remember that the gift of water is very precious."

And so it was, and still is today.

Author's Note

I first heard the story of Snail and her gift of pure water from a Navaho storyteller who had heard it from her grandmother. The tale has a simplicity and relevance for today that I find appealing. Later I found another version of the story entitled "Snail Brings Pure Water" in Franc Johnson Newcomb's book *Navaho Folk Tales* (Museum of Navaho Ceremonial Art, 1967).

The story of Snail is part of a larger Navaho creation and evolution myth. This myth describes the ascent of the Navaho people, who refer to themselves as T'áá Diné, from the lower worlds to the fifth and present world. It is part of a Navaho oral history that has been passed down from generation to generation.

The Navaho homeland consists of flat alluvial valleys, brightly colored mesas, and rolling plains. Usable water is very scarce. Farmers must use an irrigation system to grow corn, beans, pumpkins, and melons. Water, therefore, is never taken for granted.

In other versions of the story, there is a lake in the new land that contains stale, muddy water. A general search for water precedes the quest for the underwater spring. And the trickling water forms a shining brook without the help of the water chant. In retelling the tale, I chose to honor the oral tradition by following my original source, the young Navaho storyteller. Having First Man create the river from the last remaining drop of pure water is a reminder that earth's water supply is not infinite.